Wenceslaus Hollar, Sebastian Franck, Charles-Alphonse
Dufresnoy, John Bowles

The Principles of Drawing

An easy and familiar method for the improvement of youth in the practice

of that useful art - being a compleat drawing book

Wenceslaus Hollar, Sebastian Franck, Charles-Alphonse Dufresnoy, John Bowles

The Principles of Drawing
An easy and familiar method for the improvement of youth in the practice of that useful art - being a compleat drawing book

ISBN/EAN: 9783337390631

Printed in Europe, USA, Canada, Australia, Japan

Cover: Foto ©Andreas Hilbeck / pixelio.de

More available books at **www.hansebooks.com**

THE

PRINCIPLES

OF

DRAWING:

OR,

An Eafy and Familiar Method for the Improvement of Youth
in the Practice of that ufeful ART.

BEING

A COMPLEAT DRAWING BOOK:

CONTAINING

A curious Collection of Examples in all the Variety of Cafes;

As the feveral Parts of the Human Body, whole Figures, Landfkips,
Cattle, &c. curioufly Engraved on Copper-Plates, after the Defigns of
ALBERT DURER, ABRAH. BLOEMART, CARLO MORAC, LE CLERC, HOLLAR,
and other Great Mafters.

To which is prefix'd,

AN INTRODUCTION TO DRAWING;

CONTAINING

An Account of the Inftruments and Materials ufed in DRAWING, and the Method of
managing them; with Eafy and Proper LESSONS for a YOUNG BEGINNER, tending
to form his Judgment and direct his Practice.

Tranflated from the FRENCH of

Monfieur GERARD DE LAIRESSE,

And improved with Abftracts from C. A. DU FRESNOY.

The SIXTH EDITION.

LONDON:

Printed for JOHN BOWLES, at the *Black Horfe* in *Cornhill*;
and CARINGTON BOWLES, in *St. Paul's Church Yard.*

M.DCC.LXIV.

The ART of

DRAWING.

Of DRAWING in general.

DRAWING is the art of reprefenting by lines and fhades, the figure of any objeʒ we fee, or of any form we conceive an idea of in the mind.

It is a moft ingenious, ufeful and elegant art; and the ftudy of it ought to be encouraged in every youth, that difcovers an inclination or genius towards the practice thereof, whatever ftation of life he may be placed in. Its utility is fo very extenfive, there are few arts, and few profeffions in which it is not ferviceable. All defigns and models are executed by it. Mathematicians, engineers, architects, mariners, gardiners, embroiderers, weavers, and a multitude of other profeffions, have frequent occafion to practife it. In moft ftations it is ufeful, from the general who commands an army, to the mechanic who fupports himfelf by handicraft.

A perfon who has knowledge in drawing, and a capacity of performing it, ufually fees and remembers the form, fhape, and other circumftances of objeʒs, more minutely and perfect than one unacquainted with the art; and poffeffes an accomplifhment, exceedingly defirable both for amufement and ufe: he is qualified to take on the fpot the fketch of a fine building, of a beautiful profpeʒ, of any curious production of art, or of uncommon and ftriking appearances in nature, and to bring home for future infpeʒion and fervice, the forms of objeʒs which yield entertainment in journies and diftant places.

This ingenious art not only affords a very pleafing entertainment to men of leifure and fortune, in a variety of inftances, but enables them to judge the propriety of defigns, for fuch works as they intend to have executed : to lay down and exhibit their conftruction, and vary and improve the plan moft to their own liking.

Of all others, this art has the greateft number of admirers, and no wonder, fince in a kind of univerfal language, underftood by all men; it reprefents to our view, the forms of innumerable objeʒs we have no other ways of beholding : and helps us to the knowledge of many of the works in nature or art, which any other method of defcribing would be infufficient to give an idea of, It tranfmits to our view things long fince paft, and preferves the forms of others, that will foon perifh. It reprefents the deeds of people and aʒions for many ages dead; and hands down to us the features and refemblances of our anceftors, and of other valuable and renowned perfons of former generations, The efteem of this excellent art is not confined to adults; children admire it, and often by the power of a natural genius, draw a variety of objeʒs in fuch a manner as to excite commendation.

For the inftruʒion of youth in this ufeful art, the following rules are laid down, and a courfe of proper leffons exhibited for their practice.

General RULES to be obferved.

WHETHER you draw after nature, or the performances of others, the hand can only exprefs by lines and fhades, thofe forms and ideas which have impreft the mind. Hence the utility appears of accuftoming the mind to a curious and attentive obfervation of objeʒs, efpecially of thofe intended for imitation : its impreffions will hereby be ftrengthened; its conceptions will be more exaʒ and juft; and the hand will delineate with greater eafe and correʒnefs, thofe forms which are clearly and ftrongly retained in the memory.

Inform your judgment of the properties and excellencies of a drawing well executed. In this knowledge the mind will make quick improvement, by a frequent attentive infpeʒion, of the performances of thofe who have excelled. In viewing them, contemplate the freedom and boldnefs of the outline; the correʒnefs or juftnefs of the proportion of the feveral parts; the character which is peculiar and diftinguifhing in every figure, and expreffive of the circumftances it is fuppofed to be in; the elegance, or that which gives a kind of delicacy, or certain agreeablenefs which pleafes every one; the perfpeʒive, or reprefentation of the parts according to their fituation with refpeʒ to the point of fight. If the judgment be well informed in thefe particulars, the young practitioner will make much greater improvement, than can poffibly be attained, if he proceeds in practice without a due regard to increafing knowledge and judgment.

> *More to the genius than the hand we owe,*
> *From this the beauties of your art muft flow.*

The labour of the hand muft fecond and fupport that of the brain. To become an able artift, the art muft be made habitual. An eafy and juft expreffion is only to be gained by conftant practice. In all arts, the rules are learned in a little time, but the practice requires a long and fevere diligence. The hand fhould be improved in practice, and the mind in judgment every day.

Let your firft practice be employed in imitating the moft plain and fimple objeʒs : in accuftoming your hand to draw ftrait lines, perpendicular and horizontal ones; circular and irregularly curved lines. This method will be ufeful in bringing the hand to a facility of operation. Moreover, thefe lines are the rudiments of all objeʒs that can be expreffed; they bound and circumfcribe every figure; all its parts or members are compofed of them. A little time may be advantageoufly employed in drawing after plain inanimate figures, which require ftrokes of various curvings. After this draw the particular features of the face, beginning with the eye, the nofe, the mouth, the ears. Draw them in their different pofitions. Perfevere in copying feveral times after the fame example, before you make the tranfition to a new one. You cannot expeʒ to draw an entire head or face, till you are capable of performing the parts feparately; nor of copying with pleafure and improvement thofe objeʒs which require more art and time, till you have acquired a cuftomary exercife of patience, and a freedom and exaʒnefs in copying thofe that are eafier.

Sketch your outline at firft very faint, that the amendment of it may be performed without its appearing to be re-touched : endeavour at a graceful freedom, boldnefs, and juft proportion of all its parts; in thefe the excellency of a good outline confifts. It fhould be drawn with flowing and gliding ftrokes, not fwelling fuddenly, but with gradual rifings, fuch as might juft be felt in ftatues. Be careful that it lofes nothing of its freedom and boldnefs, when you correʒ it by reducing fome parts, and fwelling others. The outline on that fide neareft the light, muft be fainter than the other. The fureft and moft improving method of practice, is to fketch outlines for a confiderable time, without attempting to fhade any of them; and to make numbers of fketches from the fame pattern, imitating as nearly as you can every ftroke, and carefully to compare each of your copies with the original, that you may obferve wherein it is faulty, and avoid thofe errors in your next fketch. A good outline is of the greateft importance and extent in the art of

drawing;

drawing; an ability to make it can only be acquired by application and practice.

Proceed flowly in your firſt attempts, making it your care to ſecure every ſtroke, and rather to produce one good ſketch than in a heedleſs manner to hurry over a number of bad ones. View your original with cloſe attention; ponder upon the length, the breadth, and the form of each part; their proportions to one another, and to the whole; the diſtance from one part to the other; which of them lie parallel, and which underneath the other. In conſidering what parts are oppoſite to each other, you may conceive, or occaſionally draw, a perpendicular line from the top to the bottom, and a ſtrait line from ſide to ſide, and notice what parts are marked by theſe lines, and in what manner others deviate from them. This obſervation may be made by laying your ruler acroſs the work, and obſerving the parts interſected thereby.

Sketch out the general appearance of the whole in very faint ſtrokes, without regarding the minute particulars and little turns, theſe may be added afterwards. Review your ſketch after it has been laid aſide for ſome time, comparing it again with the original: faults may then appear which were undiſcovered before. This method of practice, tends to make you more perfect in any particular ſketch, and by improving your knowledge of outlines and proportions, to enable you for nearer imitations after other patterns.

Proportion, or the juſt magnitude of the ſeveral members of a figure, with regard to one another and the whole figure, makes one eſſential article in every good draught. A ſcheme of the proportions of a graceful human figure is given in the fifth leſſion, taken from the meaſures of antique ſtatues, eſteemed for the higheſt degrees of proportion. A knowledge of theſe will be of great ſervice to the young ſtudent, yet it muſt not be ſuppoſed, that this ſcheme is the ſtandard of meaſurement for all figures. For

Different attitudes make a ſenſible difference in the limbs of the ſame body: the muſcles ſhift their appearances, ſwelling one way and narrowing another, in different movements. Thus the arm, the foot, the knee, &c. are enlarged by bending them, and the limbs are alſo foreſhortened.

Moreover, different human bodies of agreeable appearances, have not the ſame meaſures and exact proportions in their features and limbs, therefore the eye muſt judge of gracefulneſs and proportion.

Fitneſs to peculiar characters ſhould always be joined to the idea of proportion. Brawny muſcular limbs are expreſſive of ſtrength, and more ſlender forms of agility for motion. The legs of chairmen, and the ſhoulders of watermen, are enlarged by their different occupations. Aukward as ſuch a figure appears, yet a thoughtleſs country clown is fitly expreſſed by a large head, ſhort neck, high ſhoulders, flat ſtomach, thick knees and thighs, and large feet. Proportion, in theſe and other inſtances, are regulated by fitneſs to peculiar characters, and no exact dimenſions can be given of them.

The proper materials for Drawing.

THE materials for drawing, are black lead pencils, charcoal, crayons of black, white or red chalk, or other dry colours made up into crayons; a porterayon, Indian ink, hair pencils, crow-quill pens, a ruler and pair of compaſſes.

A black lead pencil is moſt convenient at the beginning of practice. Slope your pencil to a fine point: accuſtom yourſelf to hold it further from the point than the nib of a pen in writing; this is neceſſary to an eaſy command of hand, and to the making your ſtrokes with freedom and boldneſs.

Charcoal of a fine ſmooth grain, ſlit into ſlender pieces for the porterayon, is very proper for ſketching, as any ſtrokes made with it are eaſily bruſhed out with a feather or clean ſoft rag, if you think them wrong. Having ſecured your outline with charcoal, wipe it ſlightly over with a feather, to make the lines faint, then go over them with black or red lead, endeavouring to make them more correct. Theſe new ſtrokes, when wrong, may be diſcharged with the crumbs of ſtale white bread. In ſketching after plaiſter, or academy figures, charcoal is much uſed, becauſe it is eaſily diſcharged.

Chalk, the beſt ſort of it, is free from gritdneſs and ſand, is pretty ſoft, and has a kind of fatneſs in it. Black chalk is often uſed on blue or grey paper, the colour of which ſerves for good part of the ſhading, and the lights are put in with white chalk. Red chalk is uſed on white paper: the ſhades made in hatching

with it receive a ſoftneſs, by rubbing them in gently in the broad ſtrong parts with a ſtump made of waſh leather, and then hatching upon them again. Chalk is proper for drawing large figures; but a little experience will teach you, to be careful not to make falſe ſtrokes with it, for they are very difficult to be diſcharged from the paper.

Crayons are any colours mixt with tobacco-pipe clay, which, while ſoft, and in the conſiſtency of paſte, is rolled up in pieces about the thickneſs of a quill, and two or three inches in length, and then being dried, are properly called dry colours. They work eaſieſt and expreſs themſelves ſtrongeſt on paper of a rough grain, and are uſed on coloured paper. If dark, or browniſh, or near the colour of whited-brown paper, it yields a good relief to the tender parts of the work. In uſing theſe colours they are rubb'd and wrought one into another, in ſuch a manner that no ſtrokes appear, but the colours are mixt as if they were laid in with a bruſh. Many pictures after the life are painted in crayons.

Drawing with theſe dry colours is quick and expeditious, and when the crayons are handled with judgment they give a delicate ſoftneſs; but the touch of a rude finger may ſpoil the fine work, or a damp place mildew it.

Indian ink does not ſpread and run like common ink, and the work performed with it appears much ſofter. It is bought in ſmall cakes, and by mixing it with water may be made to any degree of ſtrength, and uſed either with a hair pencil, or in a pen like common ink. When the young ſtudent has made ſome progreſs in drawing with his black lead pencil, and begins to uſe this ink, let him ſecure his outline as correct as he can with the black lead, then he may trace it over with a pen or hair pencil and Indian ink, and afterwards with the crumb of white bread rub out any remaining marks of his black lead pencil.

Shading with this ink is ſometimes done by hatching with the pen, or making ſtrokes croſſing one another; but this is as well, or better performed with the hair pencil. A more expeditious and cuſtomary manner is waſhing or working the ſhades with the ink and hair pencils, in the ſame way as water colours are uſed. The ſhades made by hatching, reſemble the ſtrokes of engraved prints. In waſhing the ſhades, they appear like thoſe in mezzintinto prints, in which there is not any lines.

The ruler and compaſſes are uſeful in making geometrical figures and in architecture; excepting in theſe inſtances the ruler is never to be uſed, and the compaſſes but ſeldom: occaſionally they may be applied in nicely examining the agreement of the copy with the original, but it is beſt to judge in moſt caſes by the eye only.

And if you would the compaſs *manage right,*
Guide it not with your hands, *but by your* ſight.

The conduct of the tints of lights and ſhadows.

IT is the proper diſtribution of light and ſhade, which gives the appearance of ſubſtance, round or flat ſhapes, diſtance, and relievo or projection, to whatever bodies you repreſent.

Draw a circle, and according to the manner in which you ſhade it, it will either receive a flat, a globular, or a concave appearance. Fill it up with an even colour, or with a number of lines of the ſame ſtrength, and it will reſemble a body with a round circumference and flat ſides. By colouring it ſtrongeſt in the middle, the edges are made to retire by the graduating ſhades, and it receives a convex appearance like a globe. By gradually weakening the ſhades from the edge towards the center, the middle part will be made to retire, and a concave appearance like a baſon be given to it.

Thoſe parts of an object which have the greateſt vivacity of colour, catch the ſight firſt and appear neareſt to it. By gradually weakening the colour, the other parts are made to recede from the eye, and appear farther off.

Pure and unmixed white, either brings an object nearer, or makes it to retire further. If the white be gradually weakened, and ſupported by a ſhade, it then advances; but unleſs it be thus forced forward, it ſhies off to the remoteſt view.

In rounding the parts of any object, the light and ſhade muſt be gradually ſoftened into one another, and loſe themſelves by ſlow and almoſt imperceptible degrees.

The outline muſt be faint in thoſe parts which receive the light, and ſtrong and bold where the ſhades fall.

Being

Begin your shading at the top, proceed downward, and go through the whole of it with a faint shade before you give the finishing to any particular part.

A balance should be preserved between the lights and shades, they serve for a repose to one another; a broad light must therefore be accompanied with a broad shade; a fainter light with a fainter shade.

Light objects must have a sufficient strength of shadow to sustain them, and dark bodies must be relieved by a mass of light behind. Without this opposition, objects will adhere to the ground, or stick to one another; but by distributing lights and shadows to advantage, they are loosened and set free, and receive a strong relievo.

Those objects or parts of objects which come forwardest to view, must have strong and smart oppositions, and the highest finishing: those that are designed to be thrown further off, must be made still weaker, and less distinct. In nature, objects appear distinct or confused, according to their nearness or distance; the features of a face, or folds of a garment, are not distinguishable the length of a street; and the innumerable leaves of a distant plantation, look like one confused mass. A more accurate, or slighter finishing, gives to objects a relative dominion over each other as to their distances: the heightening of one, chases another further from the sight which is not so minutely and strongly pencilled.

Give to every object such lights as are most proper to its supposed situation. In the open air, when the sun shines full upon objects, the lights must be strong and bold, and the shadows dark: if the sun is obscured by clouds, the light is more equal and universal, but not so strong and warm, and the shades must be fainter and more sweet. Artificial light tinges the object with its own colour, and occasions large shadows with bold extremities. Elementary light is pure, and more generally diffused, and the shadows it produces are softer. The projecting parts of objects are nearest to the light, catch it first, are brightest, and produce shades upon the lower parts. Consider from what point, and in what direction the light falls upon the object, and place all your lights and shades according to that direction: if it falls perpendicular upon a man, the top of the head is then lightest, the shoulders in the next degree so, and the lower part gradually darker: the cavities and parts that bend inwards, not receiving any direct rays, are darkest of all; and the colours are lost in them. The full force of the principal light is to be only in one part, and ought not to be crossed or interrupted with little shadows. A sudden brightness is seen, and many reflections and demy tints are produced when the force of light strikes upon silks, sattins, vessels of silver, copper, or upon other glittering objects.

The very extremity of the shadowed side of objects is seldom the darkest of all, because it almost always receives a reflection of light from adjacent bodies. Reflexes are scarce sensible, except in the shadowed parts. All reflected light is supposed to carry with it part of the colour of the body which reflects it, so that those places which receive this light have their own colour mixed or tinged with the other. Much skill and accuracy is often required in management of the reflexes, as the same place many times receives them from different objects differently coloured. Every circumstance of the colour, light, and position of each figure, and what effect each has upon the other, is to be considered, and nature pursued in all the variety of mixtures.

Nature gives a vast variety of appearances in light and shade, a curious observer of them is rewarded with high delight; and the artist with much improvement. The sky always gradates one way or another: the rising and setting sun exhibit it with astonishing beauty and perfection. The variety of forms and colours reflected in water, from the sky and clouds, from trees, houses, and other objects, are exceeding beautiful to behold. Accustom yourself to consider the different effects of light falling upon objects, its various and delightful softnings and modulations in the shades, or parts which are more or less deprived of the rays; your judgment will this way be best informed by your senses, how to represent these pleasing appearances: the proper management of which, makes one of the great divisions or branches of painting.

FIRST LESSON.

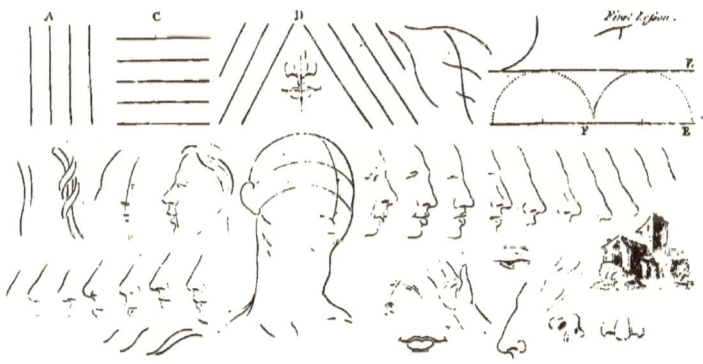

IN all arts and sciences, the learner begins with the most simple principles. The knowledge of the alphabet is an introduction to the grammar; and an ability to imitate the forms of different lines, 'tis no matter of what shape, so that they are exactly imitated, is the foundation of drawing after every kind of object.

In this first lesson the scholar is presented with many lines of different kinds for his imitation. *Viz.* Perpendicular lines marked A; that is, a line falling directly on another, so as to make equal angles on each side. C, horizontal lines which pass from one point to another without any deviation. D, oblique lines, converging or approximating one way, and diverging or continually increasing their distance the other way. E, parallel lines which are every where equidistant from each other., at F, two semicircles are drawn from points assumed in the lower line, and the upper line being a tangent to both of them, proves the truth of its being drawn parallel. Examples are also given of various sorts of curved and twining lines, &c.

SECOND.

SECOND LESSON.

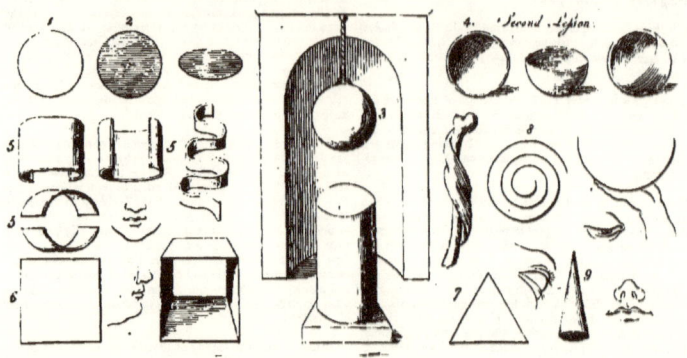

THIS second lesson consists partly of geometrical figures, some of them with plain lines, others with their surfaces formed by light and shade.

Number 1. is a circle. 2. The circle appearing with a flat side, being filled with an equal shade. 3. A convex appearance given to the circle by light and shade. 4. A concave appearance given to it. 5. Other convex and concave surfaces. 6. A square of four equal sides. 7. An equilateral triangle.

8. A spiral, or curve line issuing from a center, and continually going off from it at every turn. 9. A cone. These, with other figures shewn in this lesson, are useful in different parts of practice.

By consulting a small treatise of Practical Geometry, by Le Clerk, the student, in a short time, will gain a knowledge of the construction of geometrical figures, very advantageous in drawing multitudes of objects.

THIRD LESSON.

THIS lesson will be more pleasing to the learner than the former ones, and practising after the instances here given, will qualify him to copy more difficult representations.

FOURTH LESSON.

Directions for drawing a face.

THE following leaves exhibit many examples of the features of the human face, as the eyes, nose, mouth, ears, &c. The pupil should practise after the different features in their various positions, till he be able to draw them well : unless he can perform the parts separately, it will be fruitless to attempt the whole together.

Several easy examples are also given, of entire faces and heads, in various attitudes. When the student has made a progress in sketching after those in outline, there are others which are finished for him to shade after. By considering the plate annexed, he will improve his ideas of a face, and the method of drawing it, in all the changes and variations which are occasioned therein, by different turnings of the head,

The

The divisions and proportions of the head and face.

IN drawing a head and face, four equal parts, the length of the nose, are usually allotted from the top to the bottom. 1. From the crown of the head to the top of the forehead. 2. From thence to the top of the nose. 3. To the bottom of the nose. 4. From thence to the bottom of the chin.

The breadth of the face is divided into five equal parts; one of which parts is the length of the eye: the distance between the eyes is the measure of one part, and from the corner of the eye to the side of the face is one part. The width of the mouth is a little more than one of these parts; the width of the nose across the nostrils, a little less. The eye is divided into three parts, one of which is the measure of the pupil or sight, with the iris round it. The ear is usually the length of the nose.

These are approved proportions of a good face viewed in front, but in different beautiful subjects, the same features often vary both in length and shape.

The head in general has nearly the shape of an egg or oval as in figure 1. of the annexed plate. In the middle of the oval, draw from the top to the bottom a perpendicular line as in fig. 2. Through the centre of this line, draw another directly across, as in fig. 3. On these two lines the features of the face are to be drawn in their due proportions.

That the learner may apprehend more perfectly the use of these two lines, their variations in the different turnings of the head, and how the features on the face appear when the face is inclining to either side, turning upwards or downwards: let him either conceive of, or procure a piece of smooth wood turned in the form of an egg. Draw a line lengthways quite round the egg, as in fig. 1. and a perpendicular from top to bottom, as in fig. 2. Divide this line into two equal parts, by another which reaches from side to side, as in fig. 3. The features being drawn on these cross lines, produce a front right face, as in fig. 4. By turning the egg a small matter to the left, or to the right, the cross lines appear more curved, as in fig. 5 and 7, and the features must be drawn on them, as shewn in fig 6 and 8. The nose always projects beyond the perpendicular line, in proportion as the face is more or less turned aside, and more of the ear and nearest side of the face becomes visible. The first line which was drawn round the egg is no longer its boundary, but it gains a new circumference line, by being turned into a new position. By inclining the egg downwards, and a little to the left, the cross will appear, as in fig 9; if raised upwards, and reclining to the right, the lines appear, as in fig. 11, and the features in these instances are shewn in fig. 10 and 12. A vast variety of faces differently inclined, may be shewn by this oval or egg.

Divide the perpendicular line into four equal parts. The first must be allotted to the hair of the head. The second is from the top of the forehead to the top of the nose. The third reaches to the bottom of the nose. The fourth division includes the lips and chin. This perpendicular line divides the face breadth-ways into two equal parts: it lies exactly in the middle betwixt the eyes, runs down the midst of the nose and the gutter underneath. The middle of the mouth must always be placed on it, and the bottom of it terminates on the point of the chin.

Divide the cross line, which is the breadth of the face, into five equal parts, and place the eyes upon it, so as to leave exactly the length of one eye between them. This is to be understood of a front face, as in fig. 4. for if it turns to either side, the distance appears lessened on that side which is farthest from you. The cross line is the boundary for the top of the ears; the bottom of them is parallel with the bottom of the nose. The nostrils should not swell beyond the inner corner of the eye.

The features of a front face, when drawn upon the cross lines, according to these directions, will appear in their proper places, whatever way the oval or egg is turned, as is shewn in fig. 6, 7, 10 and 12.

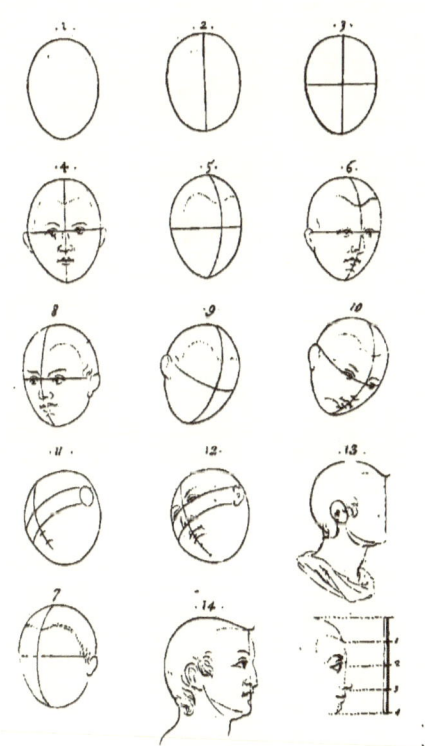

Profile, or fide faces, are to be drawn by means of a perpendicular, as in figure 13, on which the forehead, nofe, mouth, and chin are to be placed as in fig. 14. In thefe figures, the line from top to bottom is ftrictly perpendicular; it would be to in an oval drawn on paper, or any flat furface; but the curvity of an egg turns it out of that form, tho' for diftinction fake, it is defcribed by that name in the foregoing account.

When you mark the features in their proper places, touch them very lightly at firft, and afterwards proceed on them with greater exactnefs. Then draw the hair, beard, and fhadows about it. In all faces there are fome principal touches which

give fpirit, and are the characteriftic thereof; thefe fhould be well confidered, and carefully exprefs. If the face be fat, the cheeks will feem to fwell; if lean, the jaw bones will ftick out, and cheeks fall in. The corners of the mouth, and middle of the eye-brows, will be elevated in agreeable fenfations. The eye brows will rife up at the ends, and fall in the middle, and the corner of the mouth will fink in pain or uneafinefs. The mouth by fhooting forwards, and rifing in the middle, expreffes averfion. Every paffion of the foul is vifible in the features of the face; the lines and lights which are expreffive of them, claim a particular attention.

FIFTH LESSON.

The meafures and proportions of the human body.

WHEN the pupil can draw a face and head tolerably well, he may proceed upon the hands and feet. The hands are very important articles, and to perform them with eafe and freedom, is not a little difficult; much labour fhould be beftowed in practifing after the examples given of them in their various actions and forefhortnings. The hand, from the tip of the fore-finger to the wrift, is the length of a face, that is three quarters of a head; and this length is equally divided into two parts, one of which is for the palm of the hand. The thumb is the length of the nofe; the breadth of the palm is the fame as its length, equal to the length of the fore finger. The nail of the finger is about half the joint it ftands upon. The foot viewed fideways, is in length the fixth part of the figure, and may be divided into four equal parts; one of which is for the heel, two others for the fole, and the other for the toes. The great toe is commonly the length of the thumb. Thefe proportions ufually obtain, and it will be ufeful for the pupil to fix an idea of them in his mind, tho' there be few opportunities of applying them directly, becaufe of the forefhortnings in which thefe parts appear in almoft every graceful action.

The ancients commonly allowed eight heads to their figures. The moderns ordinarily divide the figure into ten faces, the face beginning at the root of the loweft hairs on the forehead, and ending at the bottom of the chin.

An human figure, divided according to this method into ten equal parts, of the length of a face, each divifion will reach as follows:
The firft, from the crown of the head to the noftrils.
The fecond, to the hole in the neck between the collar-bones.
The third, to the pit of the ftomach.
The fourth, to the navel.
The fifth, to the lower part of the belly.
The fixth and feventh, to the upper part of the knee, the thigh being the length of two faces.
The knee contains half a face.
From the lower part of the knee to the ankle, two faces.
From the ankle to the fole of the foot, half a face.

A man with his arms extended, from the extremity of the longeft finger of his right hand, to the longeft of his left, meafures as broad as he is long, *viz.*
From the tip of the long finger to the joint of the wrift, one face.
Thence to the elbow, one face and one third.

Thence to the juncture of the fhoulder, one face and one third.
Thence to the hole in the neck, one face and one third.
In all five faces, which with the five along the other arm to the tip of the middle finger, gives ten.

In meafuring a figure by eight parts, each part the length of the head, the divifions allotted to them are, *viz.* from the crown of the head to the point of the chin, one: thence to the bottom of the breafts, one: thence to the navel, one: thence to the lower part of the belly, one: thence to the middle of the thigh, one: thence to the lower part of the knee, one: thence to the fmall of the leg, one: thence to the bottom of the foot, one.

The figure with his arms ftretched out, meafured breadthways by eight parts or heads, is divided as follows, *viz.* From the end of the long finger to the wrift, one: thence to the bend of the arm, one: thence to the bottom of the fhoulder, one: thence over to the other fhoulder, two: thence to the end of the other long finger, three.

The proportions of a man differ in fome refpects from thofe of a woman; particularly the head of a woman is lefs than that of a man, and her neck longer: the breafts and belly are lower: the fpace from the bottom of the breaft to the navel, is half the length of the nofe lefs than in men, and the thigh a third part of the nofe fhorter. As to the breadth, a woman has her breafts and fhoulders narrower, and her haunches larger; her thighs at the place of articulation are larger: the tops of their arms and legs are larger than a man's, but downwards more flender, and their hands and feet are lefs.

A new born infant is not at moft above four heads long, and feldom fo much. At four or five years old it is about five heads long, and the length of the body increafes with its age, till it arrives to the ftate of manhood, and attains its full proportions.

The thicknefs of the limbs muft be adjufted agreeable to the quality and character of the figure. In general it may be noticed, that the breadth of the thigh at the thickeft, is double that of the thickeft part of the leg, and treble that of the fmalleft: but there is a difference in the contours of parts when put in different poftures. Thus when the arm is bent, it is larger than when ftraight: the fame is true of the foot and knee, and other limbs and joints.

SIXTH LESSON.

Directions for drawing the figure at full length.

BEGIN with making the oval for the head, and divide it according to the inftructions already given. Agreeable to that univerfal rule in all juft defigns of comparing and proportioning every part to the firft, the reft of your figure muft now be proportioned to the head; therefore draw a perpendicular from the top of the oval, and mark on it eight divifions or lengths of the head for the height of the figure and adjuftment of its parts. This line is alfo of ufe in placing the figure upright; and whether it be meafured by eight heads or ten faces, the former leffon directs what parts of the body are to be placed on the feveral divifions.

Sketch the head firft, then the fhoulders; then draw the trunk of the body, beginning with the arm-pits (leaving the arms till afterwards) and fo down to the hips on both fides,

being careful to obferve the breadth of the waift. Then draw that leg which the body rells upon, and afterwards the other which ftands loofe. Next draw the arms, and laft of all the hands. It is fometimes recommended to begin the fketch on the right fide of the figure, that in the procefs of the work, the performer's hand may neither hide or fhade any part of it, as it may happen in fome draughts when begun on the left fide.

To enforce a direction already given in the general rules, carefully view the original you draw after; the diftance of one feature, limb, joint, mufcle, &c. from another: their length, breadth, and turnings; their proportion to each other, and to the whole figure: which of them are directly under the other, which of them are parallel, and how they ftand fituated with regard to any part of the figure.

Preferve

Preserve a juft fymmetry and harmonious correfpondence in all the parts of the figure, by forming them in due proportions to one another; not one arm bigger or longer than the other, or of a fize ill adapted to any of the other parts. Not plump and ftrong limbs, with a fhrivelled face or decayed body, or broad Herculean fhoulders with the wafted limbs of a fkribble. Take notice of the bowings and bendings of the body, and contraft the oppofite parts anfwerable thereto. If the belly bends in, the body muft ftick out: if the knee bends out, the ham muft fall in: and fo of every other joint in the body. Sketch your outline at firft very faint, marking the general appearance and proportion of the moft confpicuous and remarkable particulars with flight touches, and afterwards introduce the minute parts by tracing it over again, correcting the firft fketch by little and little, until the whole contour be finifhed with admirable exactnefs. A fteady even light is always to be chofen, that no glare may come on the original, or on your own work.

In drawing a naked body, whatever mufcles appear, muft be expreft agreeable to the rules of anatomy. They muft not be fubdivided into fmall fections, but kept as entire as poffible: only the principal mufcles, and thofe which are of fignification to exprefs that action which is reprefented, fhould be made appear. The motion or action of the figure, muft always be confidered in drawing the mufcles; for they rife and fink, and are either lefs or more apparent according to the different motions of the body. The mufcles of the leg which fupports the body, or of an arm that lifts a weight, are fuller or more fwelled than in the leg or arm which are not fo employed. Thofe of the breaft become more or lefs vifible, by lifting up or holding down the arm.

In drawing young perfons, the mufcles muft not appear fo manifeftly as in thofe who are elder and full grown. The fame is to be obferved in fat and flefhy people, and in fuch as are very delicate and beautiful. In women and children, fcarce any mufcles at all are to be expreft, and but faintly when fwelled by a forcible action. In perfons of an hardy and robuft make, they are moft apparent.

SEVENTH LESSON.

Of Drapery.

IN cloathing your figures, or cafting the drapery over them with elegance and propriety, it fhould be confidered, that the beauty of draperies confift not in the multitude of folds, but in their natural order and plain fimplicity. 1. The drapery muft encompafs the parts loofely; when it fits too ftrait or clofe, it gives a ftiffnefs to the figure, and feems obftructive to its motions. 2. Draw the plaits large, and following the form of the limbs underneath, that they may be diftinguifhed from others by a due management of the light and fhades. The extremities of the joints, as the fhoulders, elbows, knees, &c. fhould be fo marked as to be apparent, as far as art and probability will permit, notwithftanding they are covered. This is fo material a confideration, that many artifts firft fketch the naked figure, and afterwards put the drapery on it. 3. The great folds muft be drawn firft, and afterwards broke and divided into leffer ones; and great care be taken that they do not crofs one another improperly. 4. Tho' in general the folds fhould be large, and as few as poffible, yet they muft be greater or lefs, according to the quality of the ftuff of which the drapery is fuppofed to confift; fome, as coarfe woollens make their folds abrupt and harfh, and others, as filks and fine linnens more foft and eafy: the furface of fome has a luftre, others are dull; fome are pliable and tranfparent, others ftrong and folid. The quality of the perfon is likewife to be confidered in the drapery. If they are megiftrates or dignified perfonages, their robes or draperies fhould be large and ample; if ladies and nymphs, thin, foft, and pliable; if country clowns, ordinary people or flaves, they ought to be ftout and coarfe. 5. Suit the garment and folds to the pofture of the body, and the fway or action of the limbs, crooked or ftrait, or bending one way or another, according to their various pofitions, in fuch manner as will beft exprefs their attitude and motion. Different poftures and motions vary the folds, and bring them into new forms; and whatever pofture the body is fuppofed to be in, fhould be expreft by an artful complication of them; when they are well imagined, they give much fpirit to every action. 6. A great lightnefs and motion of the drapery, are only proper for figures in great agitation, or expofed to the wind. The loofe apparel in this cafe muft all fly one way, and that part of the garment which adheres clofeft to the body, fhould be drawn before the loofe part which flies from it, in order to fecure the true pofition of the figure. 7. The clofer the garment fits to the body, the narrower and fmaller muft be the folds. 8. The draperies which cover thofe parts that are expofed to great light, muft not be fo deeply fhaded as to feem to pierce them; nor fhould the limbs in that fituation of light be croffed by folds that are too ftrong, left the great darknefs of the fhade give them the appearance of being broke. 9. Whenever the drapery is adorned with rich ornaments, they fhould be introduced with judgment and priety, fuitable to the character of the figure, and is generally ufed fparingly. It is altogether improper and d... them in the imaginary reprefentation of ange... grandeur of whofe draperies, ought rath... flow of the folds, than in rich ftuff and... glitter or...

2 **EIGHTH**

EIGHTH LESSON.

Rules for drawing after models or statues.

ALWAYS chufe a north light if poffible, becaufe it is fteady and moft equally diffufed. Darken with the fhutters all the windows of the room but one, and darken the lower part of that window. The light contracted in this manner, and only admitted at an altitude above the pofition of the figure, will make the fhadows diftinct, and fhew every part of it to advantage. If you are conftrained to a window which has a fouth afpect, a tranfparent fafh of oil'd paper will moderate the light, and take off the glare.

Sit at a diftance from the model, in proportion to its fize; fo far that you may fee the whole of it at once, which may be effected at a diftance about twice or three times its magnitude. Seat yourfelf in fuch a manner, as to bring your eye upon a level with the figure.

The obfervations heretofore laid down, are applicable to this branch of drawing, to urge the moft material of them. 1. Copy after good originals. 2 Mark out all the parts before you begin to fhadow. 3. Make the contours in great pieces, without taking notice of the little mufcles and other breaks. 4. Obferve every ftroke as to its perpendicular, parallel, and diftance; and particularly fo to compare, and oppofe the parts that meet upon, and traverfe the perpendicular, as to form a kind of fquare in the mind, which is the great and almoft the only rule for producing a juft and exact copy. 5. Carefully regard not only the model you are copying after, but alfo the part you have already drawn; there being no poffibility of preferving ftrict juftnefs in your performance, but by comparing and proportioning every part to the firft.

NINTH LESSON.

Directions for copying after paintings.

PLACE your picture in a good light, by which is meant, not only an even fteady light, as directed in the former article, but alfo the proper light for the picture, that it may fall thereon either on the right or left fide, agreeable to the lights and fhadows in the painting. Seat yourfelf at a proper diftance from it, fo fee the whole picture at once. 1. Obferve nicely what object is placed in the middle of the picture; mark flightly the middle of your paper, and give it the fame fituation. 2. Obferve the principal objects on the left and on the right fide, how they are placed and ranged; fketch their rough form very flightly in the fame difpofition and proportion, till all the principal parts are marked on your paper in their proper places. 3. The expreffion or fuppofed character and circumftances of every object in the picture, muft be well ftudied and imprinted on your mind; its attitude, pofture and gefture preferved in your copy; and thofe parts be particularly noticed, by which the action and fentiment are reprefented in a ftrong and lively manner. 4. As the whole compofition fhould be flightly fketch'd before you begin to finifh any part, fo in the fhading you fhould go on with the whole together with a faint fhade, before you finifh any part. Many directions are given in the preceding effay for the lights and fhades.

A common method of adjufting the diftances, the fituation and proportion of every object agreeable to the picture, is to divide it into little fquares, and then to divide the paper for the copy into the fame number of fquares, and to draw in them

what is correfpondent to each fquare. This is a fure method to enlarge or reduce a draught with exactnefs; but if the ftudent accuftom himfelf to practife by the help of thefe fquares, he will certainly ftint and confine his judgment; let him rather help it by imaginary lines, than cramp it by real ones. Let him conceive in his mind a perpendicular and an horizontal line interfecting each other in the middle of the picture, and obferve what objects are croffed by them; and then fuppofe two fuch lines croffing his paper, in order to give thofe objects a fimilar fituation. In the like manner the fituation and proportion of all the chief parts throughout the picture may be confidered, by imagining other lines traverfing them, and dividing as it were the feveral parts of the painting into fmall fquares. The primary qualification in the art of drawing, is a readinefs of comparing and meafuring by the eye all the parts of a compofition, and an ability to exprefs them with boldnefs and juftnefs. This effential accomplifhment is to be acquired by habit and application.

The proportion, form, and magnitude of objects, their diminution in fize and luftre, are governed by the rules of perfpective. A knowledge in the practical part of that fcience, will greatly advance the pupil's judgment and facilitate his practice; and this knowledge may be attained with furprizing eafe, by confulting that plain and familiar treatife, the Jefuit's Perfpective, tranflated by Ephraim Chambers.

TENTH LESSON.

For drawing landfkips or rural fcenes after nature.

HAVING fixt your ftation, and determined what extent of view to delineate, draw the horizontal line faintly, and mark it into three divifions, then divide in your mind the landfkip into three divifions likewife. Sketch the middle divifion firft, then that on the left hand, afterwards that on the right. Obferve, 1. What objects fall under one another, and mark them on your paper accordingly. 2, What objects range on a level with each other between the two fides, and place them parallel in your draught. 3. Remark what objects are

feen through the intervals of other particular objects, and give them the fame apparent fituation. 4. Endeavour to fketch all the objects in their proportional magnitudes and diftances; they gradually diminifh as they are farther removed from the eye, and it is this diminution with gradual foftenings and indiftinctnefs, which gives diftant objects their remote appearance. There are certain infallible rules in perfpective for the management of this important article. 5. Make all your lights and fhades fall one way.

ADVERTISEMENT.

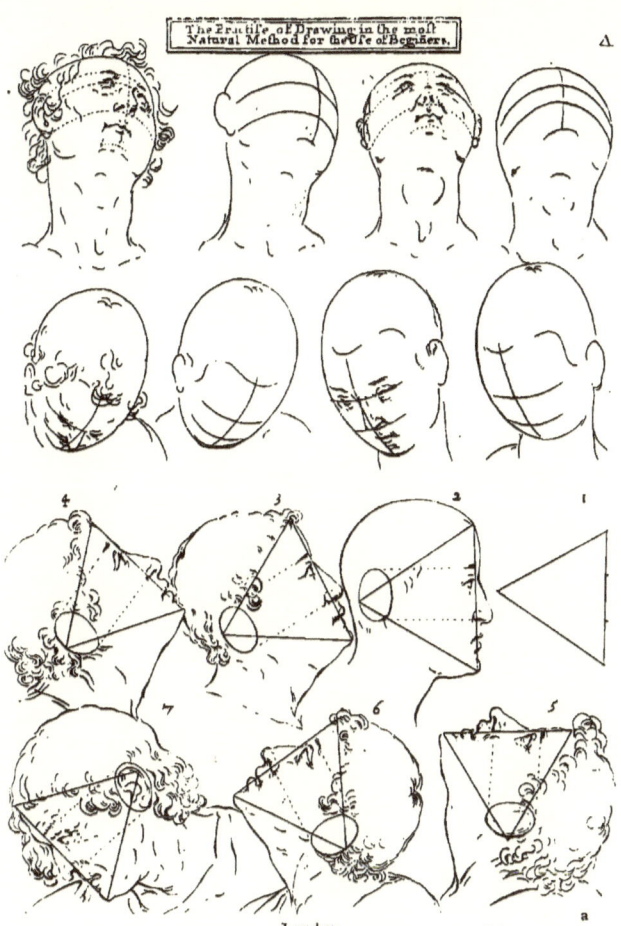

The Pratife of Drawing in the moſt
Natural Method for the Uſe of Beginners.

London
Sold by I. Bowles ____ at the Black Horſe in Cornhil.

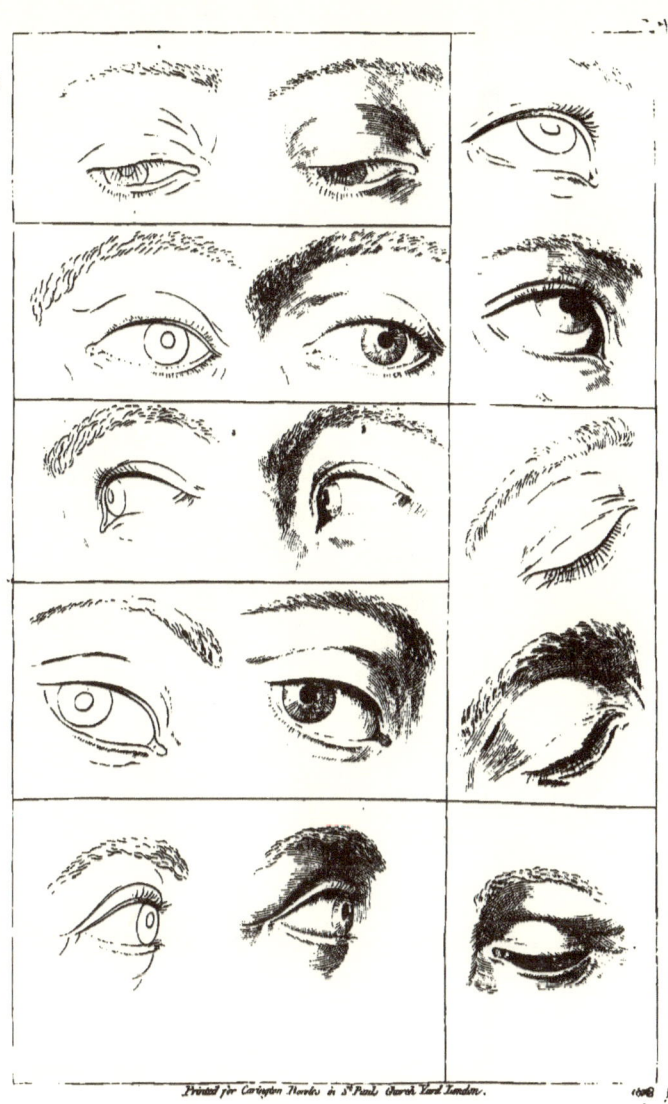

Printed for Carington Bowles in S.t Paul's Church Yard London.

Printed for Carington Bowles in St Pauls Church Yard London.

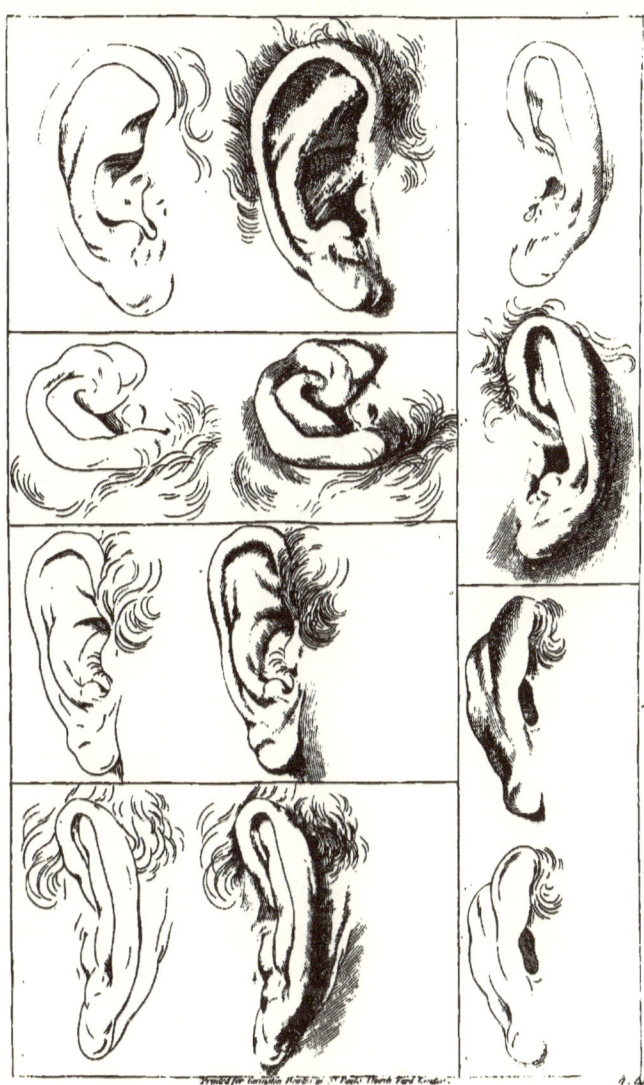

Printed for Laurence Hinde at St Paul's Church Yard London

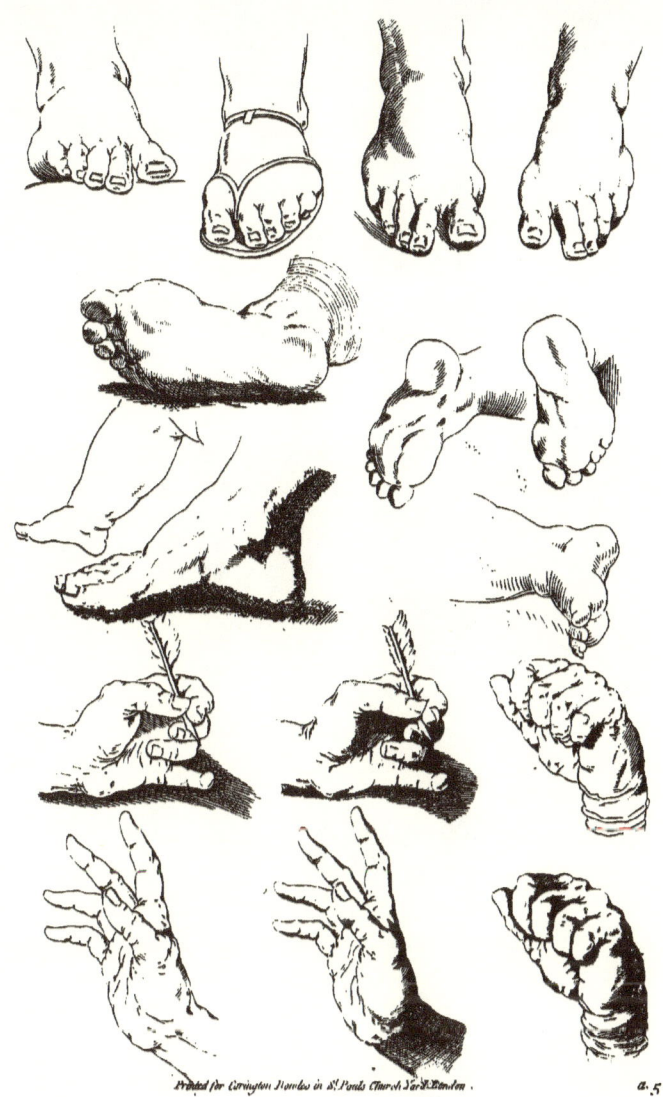

Printed for Carrington Bowles in St Pauls Church Yard London.

a. 5

F

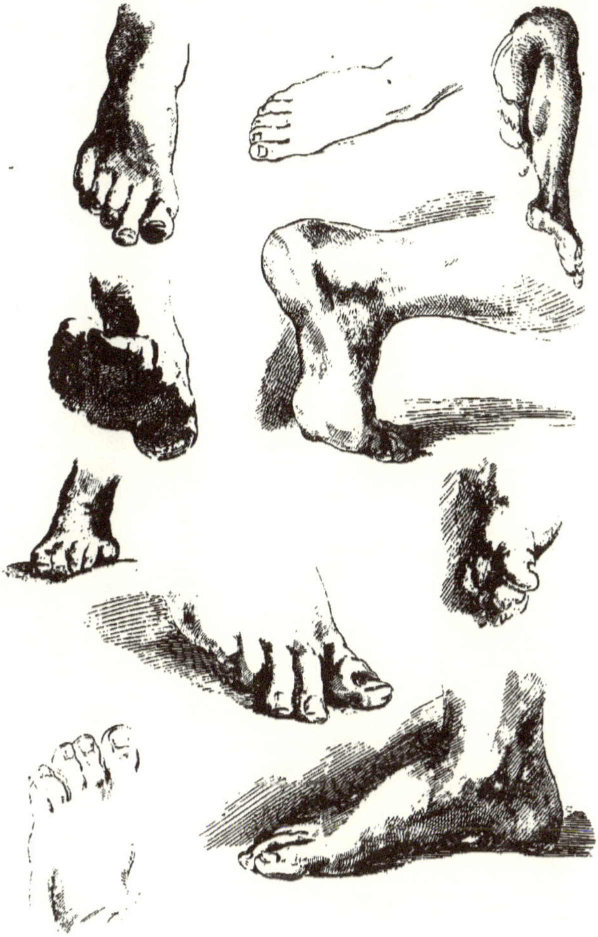

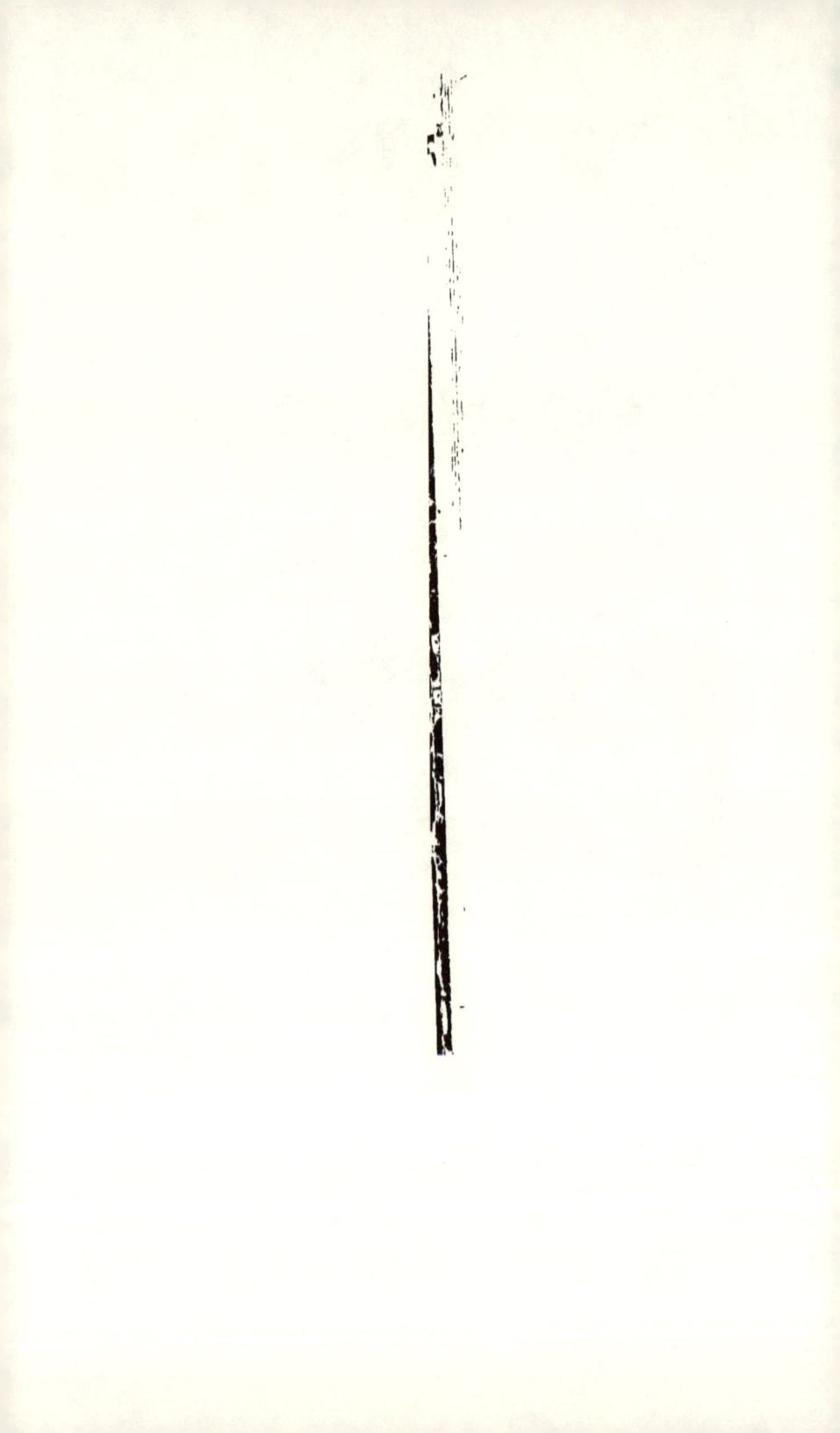

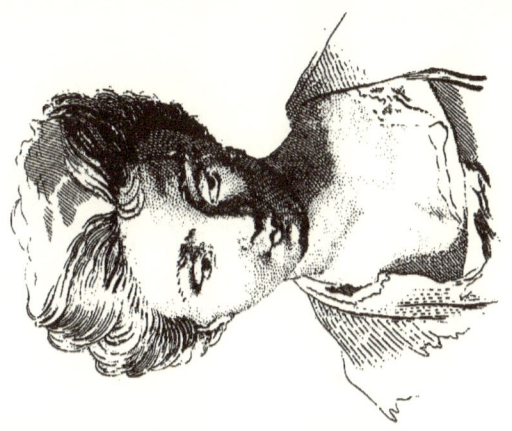

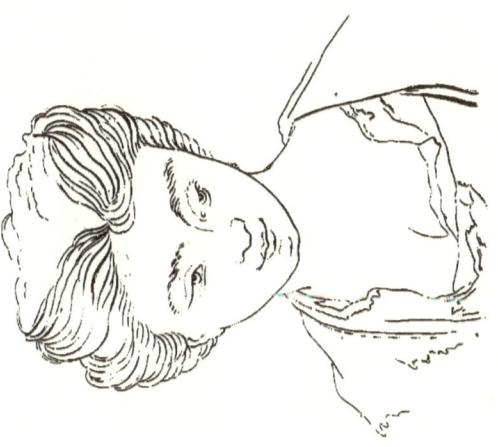

M.3.^{d}

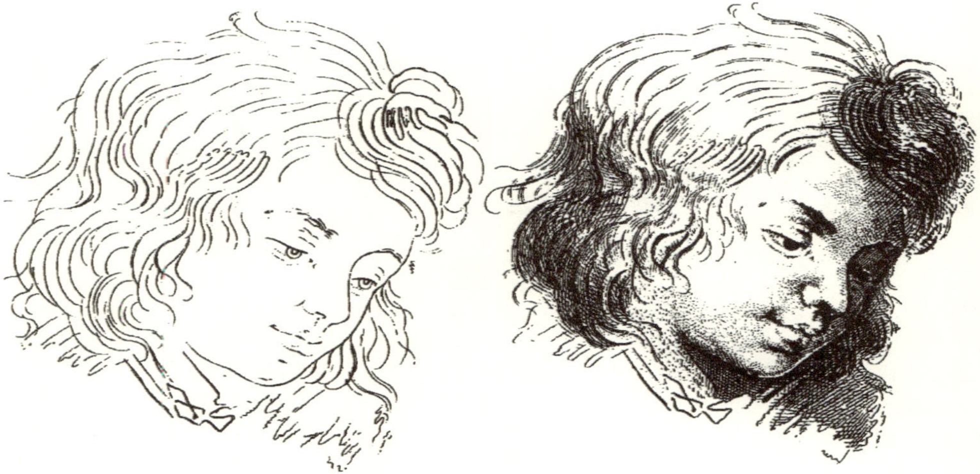

N

Printed for Carrington Bowles in St Pauls Church Yard.

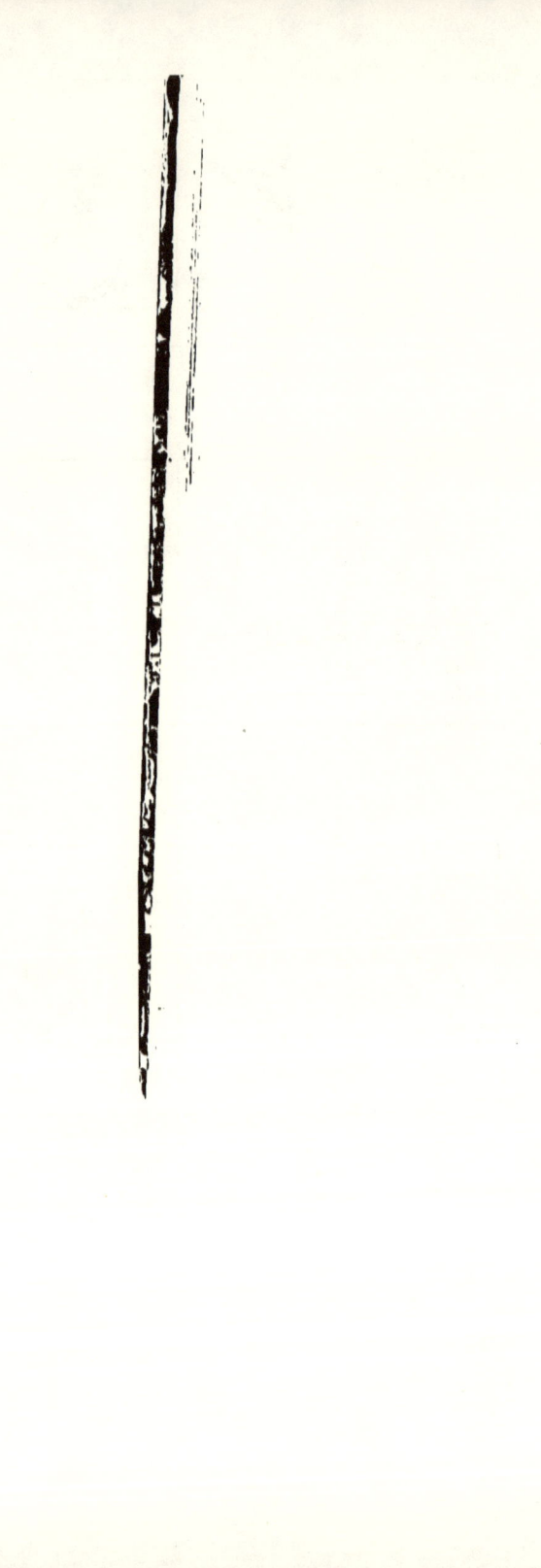

P

Printed for Carrington Bowles in S. Pauls Church Yard

Q

Printed for Carington Bowles in S.t Pauls Church Yard

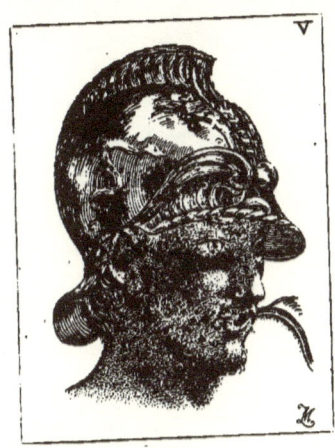

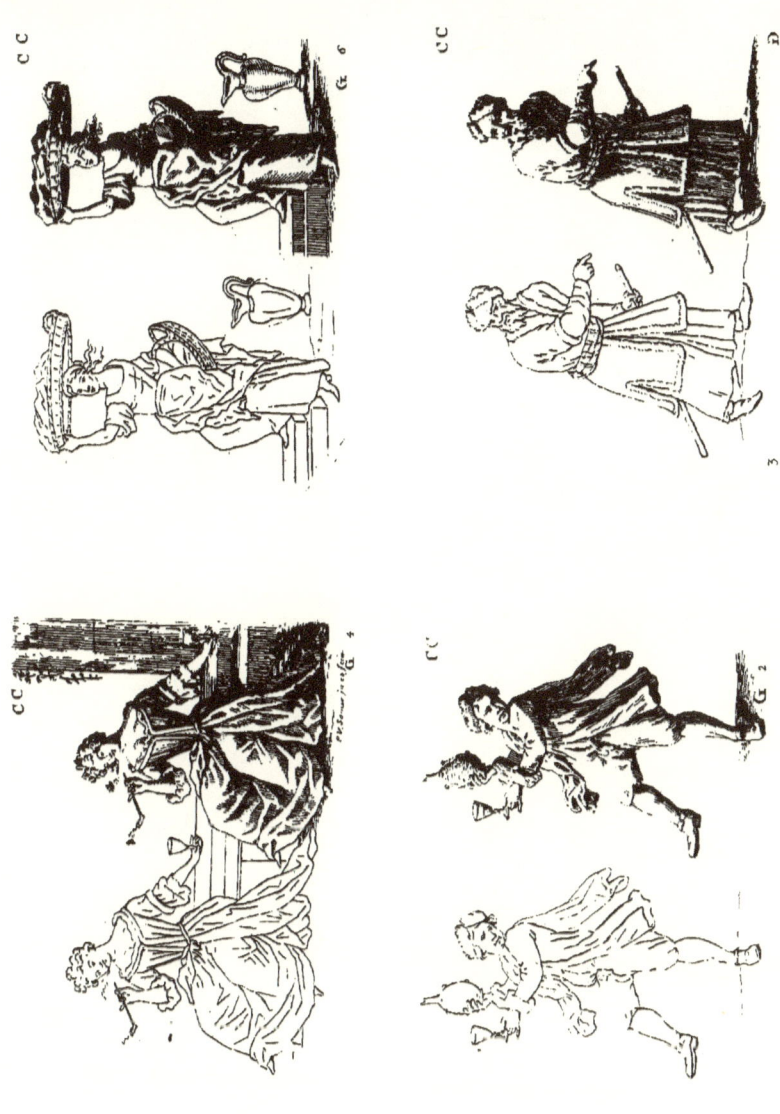

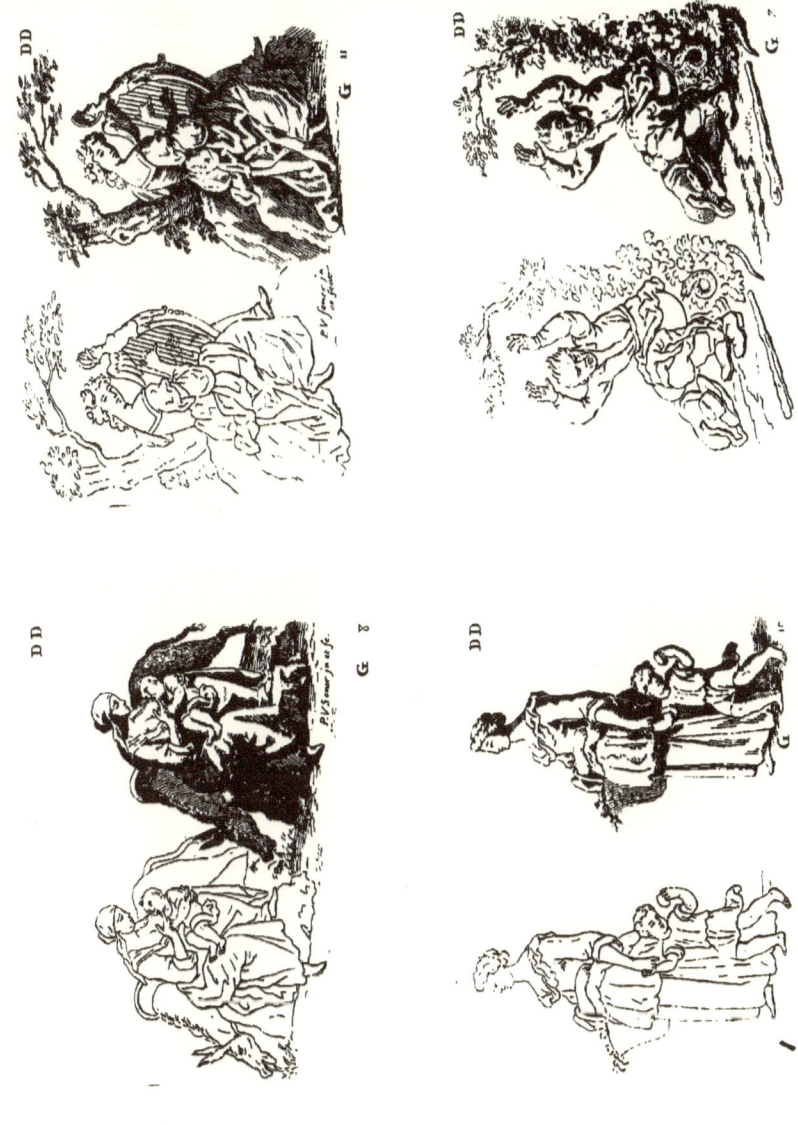

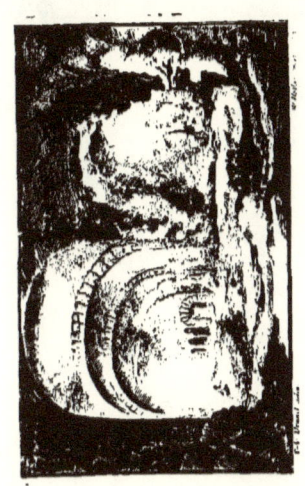

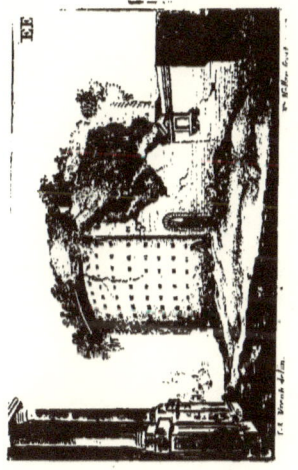

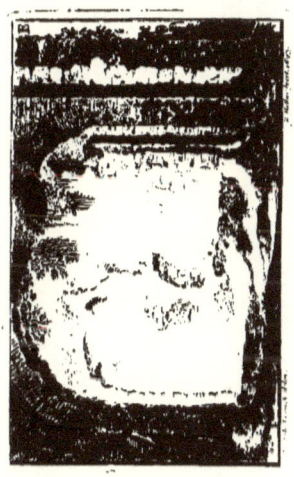

Printed for Carington Bowles in S.t Pauls Church Yard.

Printed for Carington Bowles in St Pauls Church Yard.

Printed for Carington Bowles in St Pauls Church Yard

Printed for Carington Bowles in St Pauls Church Yard.

Printed for Carrington Bowles in S.t Pauls Church Yard.

Printed for Carington Bowles in S.t Pauls Church Yard.

Printed for Carington Bowles in St Pauls Church Yard.

Printed for Carrington Bowles in S.t Pauls Church Yard.

Printed for Carington Bowles in St Pauls Church Yard.

Printed for Carington Bowles in St Pauls Church Yard.

Printed for Carrington Bowles, in St Pauls Church Yard.

Printed for Carington Bowles in S.t Pauls Church Yard.

C. Vanlo del.   F. Vivares f.

Boucher del   F. V.

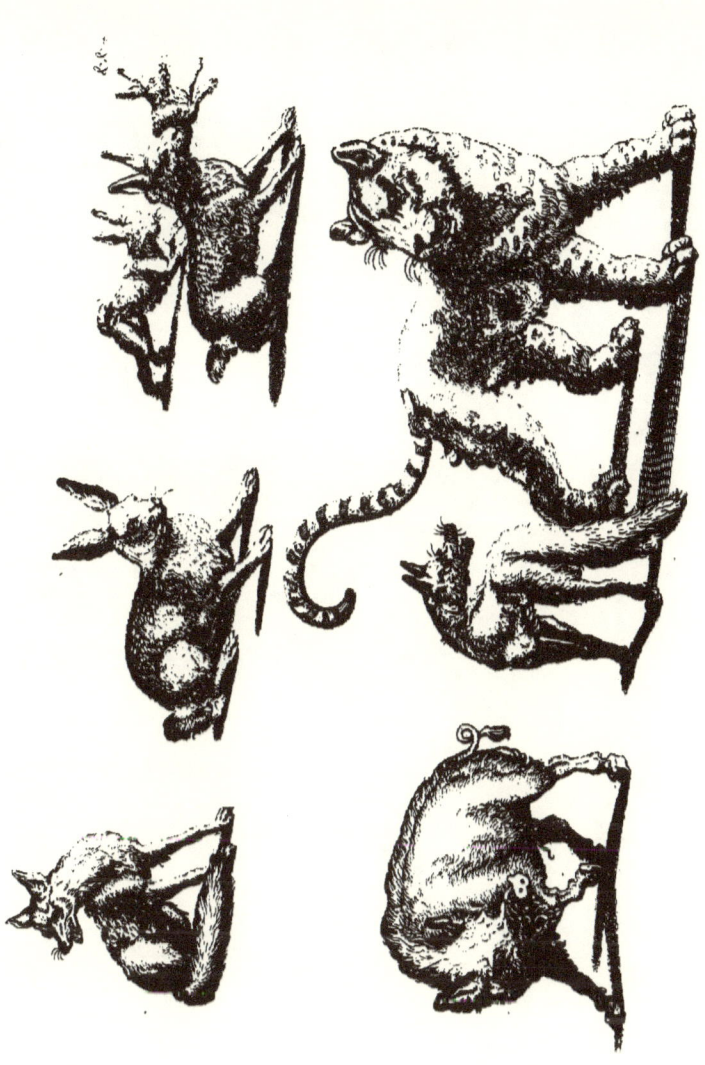

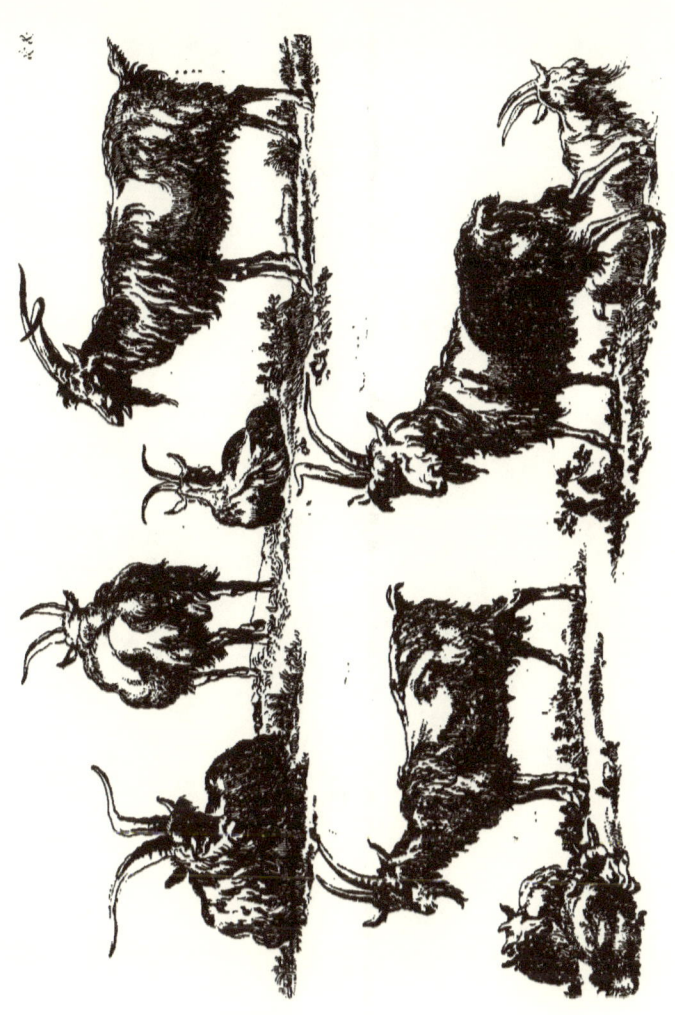

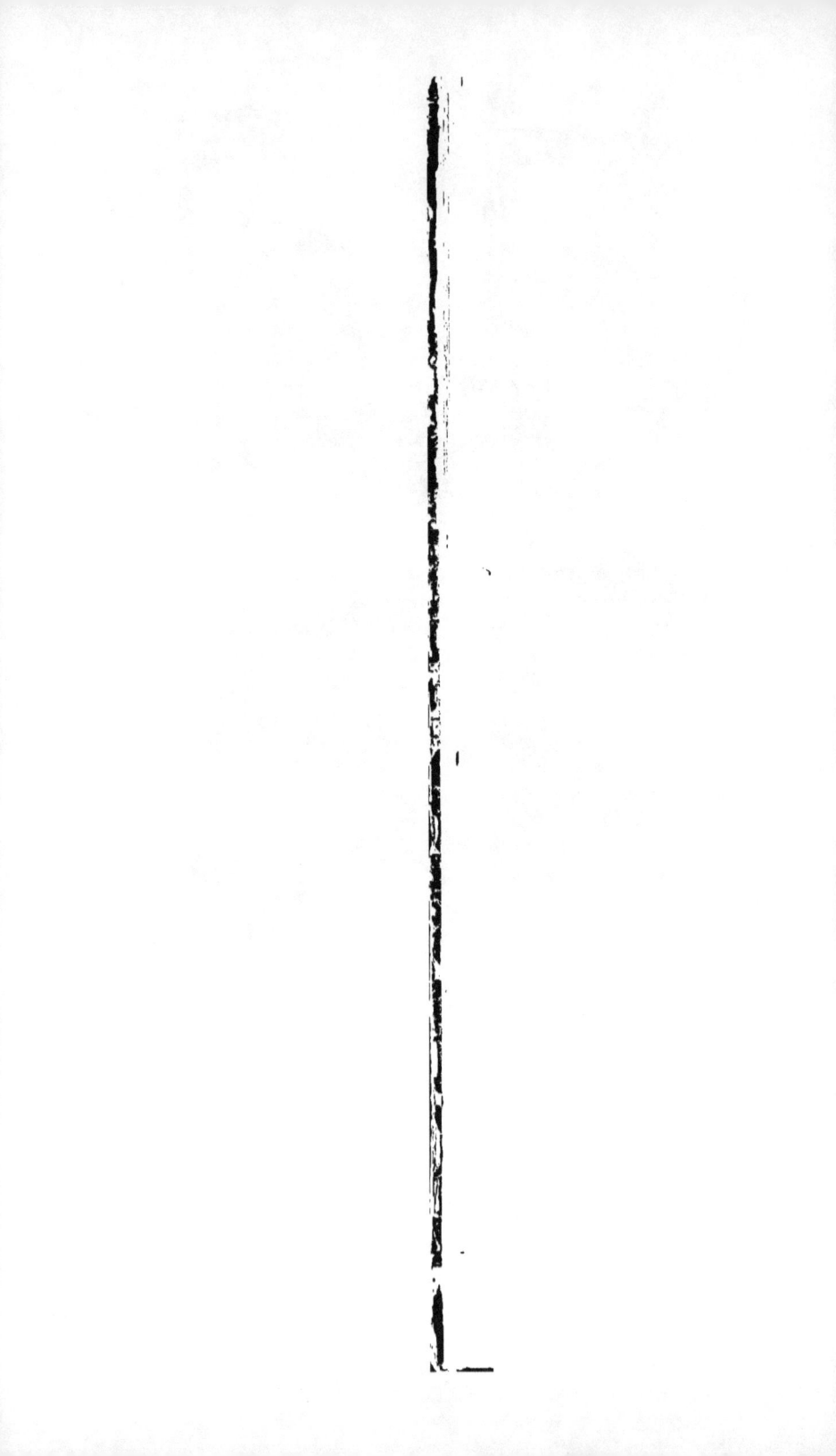